Mr Beast

For Charlie, J. S.

For Greta, Emilio and Loveday,
from Grumpy Trousers, R. A.

First published in hardback in Great Britain by HarperCollins Children's Books in 2004

1 3 5 7 9 10 8 6 4 2

ISBN: 0-00-710393-X

Text copyright © James Sage 2004
Illustrations copyright © Russell Ayto 2004

Visit our website at: www.harpercollinschildrensbooks.co.uk

Printed and bound in Singapore

Mr Beast

James Sage

illustrated by Russell Ayto

HarperCollins *Children's Books*

Charlie loved monsters almost as much as he loved sugared doughnuts. Which is why his mum said to him one day: Charlie my pet, if I had a larger frying pan, I'd make some of your favourite sugared doughnuts. Go and ask Mr Beast if I can borrow his big old black one.

So Charlie set off down the garden.

With pleasure! gushed Mr Beast,

picking his ugly sharp teeth with a

twing and a **twang**

But tell your dear mother that I

expect to have my big old black

pan returned filled to the brim

with her delectable doughnuts!

So Charlie lugged the frying pan home and his mum made him as many doughnuts as he could eat (which was a lot!).

Then she made a batch for Mr Beast which Charlie lugged back.

But on the way, Charlie began to eat these doughnuts, too...

and he kept on eating them...

until there was only one pathetic

little doughnut left.

And then he ate

THAT!

It's my sweet tooth, explained
Charlie. But such a lame excuse
did not satisfy Mr Beast.

You've eaten all my doughnuts,
bozo, so tonight I'll eat you!
Depend upon it!
And then he slammed the door
with a BANG!

When Charlie told his mum that Mr Beast was planning to eat him, she said she was very sorry indeed to hear that as she would miss him terribly but would try not to fret.

Then Charlie went through the house...

...and checking to see that Mr Beast...

...locking all the doors...   and shutting all the windows...

...wasn't already lurking in the broom cupboard, or hiding behind the fish tank.

Not long afterwards Charlie went to bed… but not to sleep! For it was then that Mr Beast came visiting, just as he said he would!

I'm going to eat you up,
Charlie boy, he called.
I'm outside now!

Shuffle
Rumble
Grunt!

And Charlie could hear
Mr Beast clambering up
the creeper!

Crickle

Crackle

Crunch!

And then Charlie could hear
Mr Beast clattering about
on the roof!

Piddle

Paddle

Plunk!

I'm coming to
eat you up,
yes I am!

And then Charlie could hear
Mr Beast stuffing himself
into the chimney!

Squiggle
Shimmy...

And then sliding down it!

swish
Slither...
SLUMP!

Now I'm in the house and I'm really going to eat you up! he shouted.

And Charlie could hear
Mr Beast stomping
along the hall!

Then Charlie heard
Mr Beast kick open the
bedroom door with one
mighty thrust of his
great big foot!

And walk right in!

Blim

Blam

BLUMP!

And when Charlie heard this he did what any brave person would do in the circumstances. He made himself as little as possible.

YEEEhaw!

howled Mr Beast as he yanked
back the bedcovers. And now I
really and truly will EAT YOU UP!

And he tickled Charlie all over
while roaring in a very
beastly voice, YUM!
YUMMY! YUM!
As Charlie shouted,
BUT IT'S ONLY
ME, DADDY,
IT'S ONLY
ME!

Such a racket naturally brought
Charlie's mum hurrying upstairs.
And this is only me to tell you
both that's quite enough silliness
for one evening! she announced.

She told Charlie's daddy to act
his age if he possibly could, as
it was already way past
Charlie's bedtime…

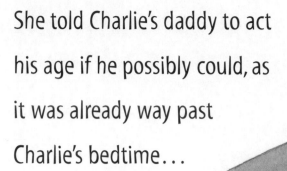

...and Charlie to stop dwelling on sugared doughnuts and go to sleep without delay!

And they both promised to be as good as gold from that moment on.

And do you think they

really meant it?